What We Wear

Diane James & Sara Lynn

Illustrated by Joe Wright

2	Work & Play	18	Rubber
4	Warm & Woolly	20	Fun Clothes
6	Pom-poms	22	Guess Who!
8	Cool Cotton	24	Dress It Up
10	Print It!	26	Beads
12	Silk Spinning	28	Cover Up
14	Fabrics	30	Quiz
16	Paper Weaving	32	Index

A **TWO-CAN** BOOK
published by
THOMSON LEARNING
New York

Work & Play

Clothes protect our bodies. We wear warm clothes in winter and cool clothes in summer. Different fabrics suit different climates.

People who do dangerous jobs often wear special protective clothing, such as helmets and gloves.

All over the world, people love dressing up in bright costumes to celebrate special occasions.

We are going to look at where different fabrics come from and at some of the clothes people wear for work and play.

Warm & Woolly

One of the warmest, softest fabrics comes from sheep. Once a year sheep are brought in for clipping. A sheep shearer holds the sheep gently between his legs and clips the woolly coat off. An expert can clip about 250 sheep in one day!

When the wool has been washed it is very tangled. The clean wool is passed through rollers with tiny wire teeth, which untangle it.

Then the wool is put into machines that twist and spin it into long lengths of yarn. Later, it is knitted or woven into fabric.

The wool that comes off the sheep's back is very dirty. It has to be washed thoroughly with soap and hot water. Then it is rinsed, squeezed through rollers, and dried.

There are lots of different kinds of sheep. Some have long, shaggy coats and some short, curly coats. Because wool is a warm fabric it is used for winter clothes, such as sweaters, gloves, scarves, and hats.

Pom-poms

Try making some of these woolly pom-poms to decorate your winter clothes.

Get ready...
Cardboard
Yarn (different colors)
Scissors

2 Put one circle on top of the other. Wind some yarn into a small ball and wrap it around and around the cardboard circles. Keep going until the hole in the middle has almost disappeared. You could use different colors of yarn.

Get set, go!
1 Cut two circles the same size from a piece of cardboard. You could use the ones here as a guide. Ask a grown-up to help you cut a small circle in the middle of each of them.

3 Ask a grown-up to help cut through the layers of yarn at the edge.

4 Tie a piece of yarn around the middle of the pom-pom between the two pieces of cardboard. Pull the cardboard circles away from the pom-pom.

You could use your pom-poms to decorate a woolly hat, sweater, or scarf.

Cool Cotton

Cotton is a cool, crisp fabric made from the cotton plant. It is light and soft and especially good for summer clothes.

The cotton seed pods can be picked by machine or by hand. A different machine cleans and dries the pods and presses them into huge bundles. These are sent to a factory where they are spun into thread.

Cotton plants grow best in sunny places. After the plant has flowered, seed pods form. When they ripen they look like fluffy, white cotton balls.

The cotton thread on the reels above is used for sewing. Other cotton thread may be made into fabrics like the ones below. The fabric can then be made into clothes.

In hot countries, people often wear long, flowing cotton robes to protect them from the fierce heat.

Print It!

Get ready...
Cardboard
Thin sponge
Cotton T-shirt
Fabric paints
(make sure
you read the
instructions on
the paints)

Get set, go!

1 Draw a simple pattern on a piece of paper and decide what colors to use.

2 Ask a grown-up to cut the sponge into the shapes that make up your pattern. Glue each piece of sponge to a piece of cardboard.

3 Use a brush to cover one of the sponge shapes with paint. Press the shape down onto the shirt. Lift it off, holding the cardboard.

4 Do the same thing with the other shapes, using different colors for each one.

Silk Spinning

Silk is soft and very strong. It is spun by silkworms. A silkworm is a special kind of caterpillar.

Silkworms have huge appetites and feed on leaves from the mulberry tree. About six weeks after hatching, a silkworm spins a web. It spins for about three days, making a cocoon the size of a pecan around itself.

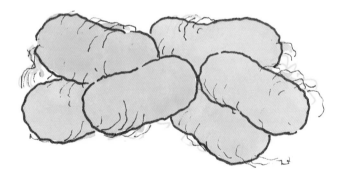

Silk workers unwind the threads of the cocoon. One cocoon can give over half a mile of silk thread!

Silk is a good fabric to wear in hot countries because it is cool and light. This Indian woman is wearing clothes made from brightly colored silk. She has wrapped a piece around her head and shoulders.

Silk is often used to make clothes for special occasions. This young Chinese boy is wearing a silk robe embroidered with dragons. Just think how busy the silkworms must have been to spin enough thread to make this beautiful costume!

Fabrics

Wool, silk, and cotton threads are all used to make fabrics. They are either woven or knitted into long pieces. The cardboard weaving loom below shows how threads are woven in and out of each other to make a piece of fabric. Weaving can be done by hand or by machine. Huge machines can produce fabric very quickly – it is much slower by hand!

Colored yarns can be woven into complicated patterns. The woman in the picture below is weaving a piece of fabric. The leather strap keeps her loom in position.

Look at the knitting on the needle here. You will see that knitted fabric is made up of a series of loops. Different colors have been used to make stripes. Knitting can also be done by hand or machine.

Knitted fabrics stretch more than woven ones. They are good for sweaters. The neck stretches to allow your head through, and then it goes back to its original shape! Knitted fabrics are also good for sports clothes because they allow you to move easily.

Paper Weaving

See how weaving works by doing it yourself.

Get ready...
Colored paper
Scissors

Get set, go!

1 Take a rectangle of paper and fold it in half. Cut slits at equal distances from the folded edge to within about an inch of the outside edge.

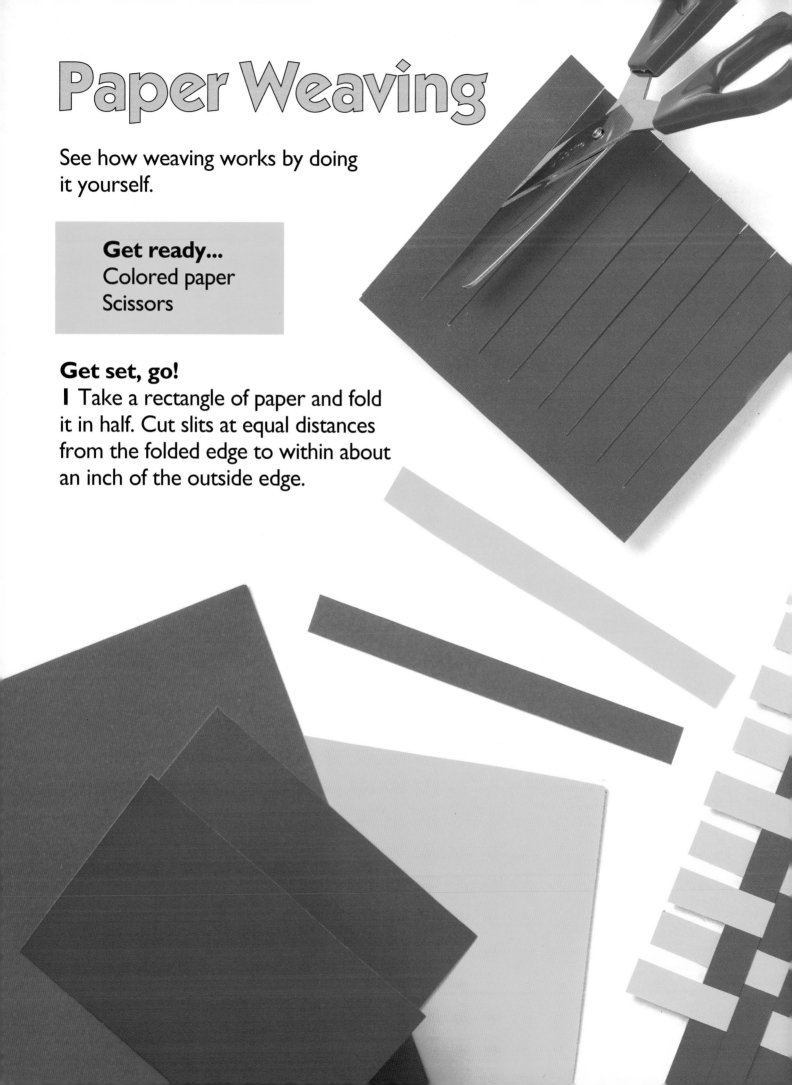

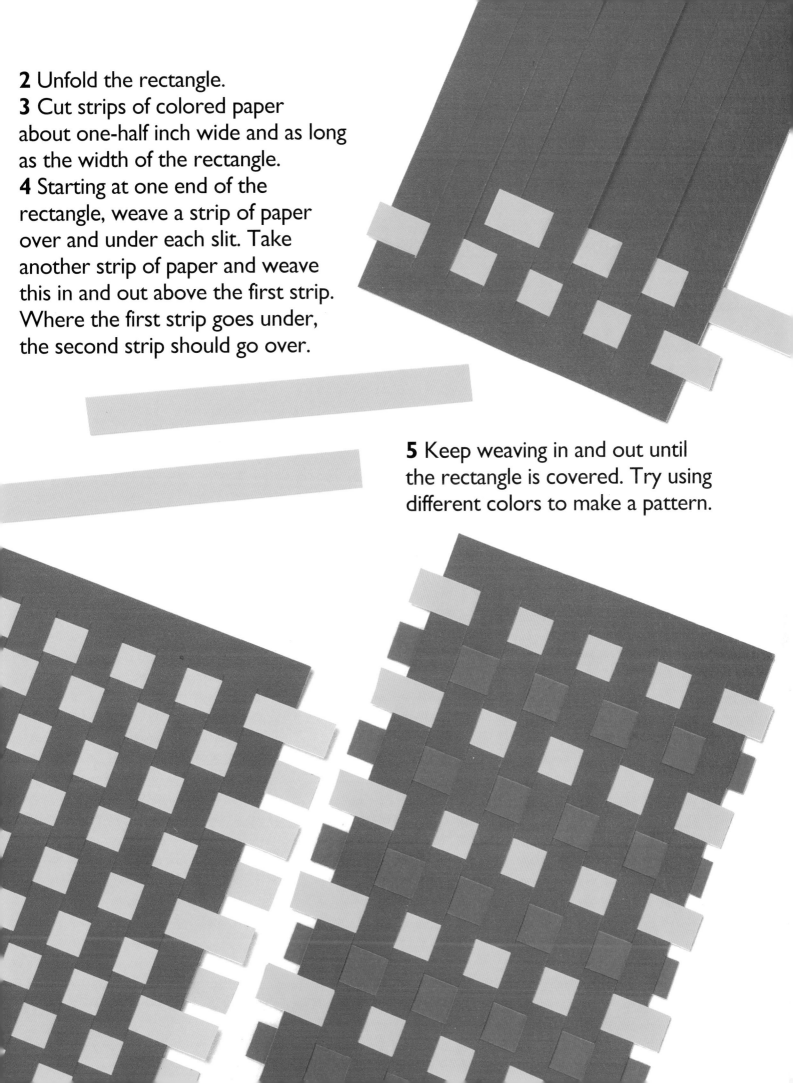

2 Unfold the rectangle.

3 Cut strips of colored paper about one-half inch wide and as long as the width of the rectangle.

4 Starting at one end of the rectangle, weave a strip of paper over and under each slit. Take another strip of paper and weave this in and out above the first strip. Where the first strip goes under, the second strip should go over.

5 Keep weaving in and out until the rectangle is covered. Try using different colors to make a pattern.

Rubber

What do you wear when it is raining to keep you dry? Some people wear rubber boots and a rubber coat. Rubber is a very useful material. It stretches, is waterproof, is airtight, and lasts for a long time.

When the bark of the rubber tree is cut, a white juice oozes out. It is caught in bowls strapped to the trunk. The juice is called latex and can be made into rubber.

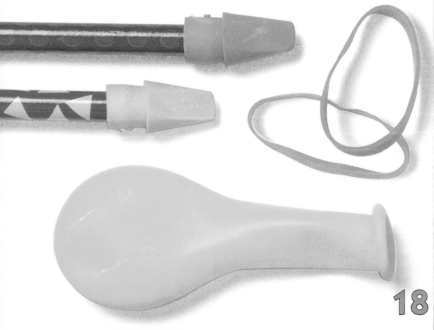

Hundreds of years ago, Indians in South America discovered a great way to protect their feet.

They spread latex from rubber trees on their feet and let it dry. This made a type of rubber shoe.

Rubber is used to make rubber bands and balloons. Balls are often made from rubber. It makes them bounce!

Fun Clothes

Sometimes people dress up for special occasions. They may be actors taking part in a play, or dancers putting on a performance. They may be going to a wedding, or perhaps a party! Do you ever dress up?

In some countries, people dress up in national costumes. The people below are wearing traditional Dutch clothing.

People spend days and days making colorful costumes to wear for festivals and carnivals. This amazing dragon was made to celebrate Chinese New Year.

This beautiful head-dress and funny mask completely hide the dancer wearing them. If you would like to make your own mask, look at the next page!

Guess Who!

The next time you have a party, why not ask your friends to wear masks? You could give a prize for the best one! Here is one for you to make.

Get ready...
Colored paper or thin cardboard
Scissors
Glue
String

Get set, go!
1 Cut out an oval shape like the one on the page opposite. Ask a grown-up to help you cut two holes for your eyes.
2 Cut different shapes from colored paper and glue them onto your mask.
3 Make a small hole at each side of the mask and poke some string through. Tie the string at the back of your head to keep the mask in place.

Dress It Up

Even the plainest clothes can be made to look exciting. You can wear brightly colored jewelry, such as necklaces and bracelets.
Or you can decorate your clothes with beads and shiny sequins. Hats, gloves, and bags can also be used to brighten up an outfit. Look at page 26 to get some ideas for making your own jewelry.

In Africa people make beautiful beaded headdresses and necklaces by hand. They must feel heavy to wear!

These girls from Thailand have beads and silver ornaments sewn on to their clothes. The flowers on their hats are made from pieces of brightly colored yarn.

Beads

Get ready...
Clay (look for the type that
   hardens in the air)
Macaroni
Flour
Salt
Water
Paint and paintbrush
String
Toothpick or knitting needle
   (for making holes through
   beads)

clay

Get set, go!
Clay Beads
1 Roll a piece of clay into a long
sausage shape.
2 Cut off small pieces and roll them
into small balls to make beads.
3 Poke a hole through the middle
of each bead.
4 Let the beads dry and harden, then
paint them bright colors.
5 Thread the beads onto a piece
of string.

Get set, go!
Macaroni Beads
1 Paint dry macaroni pieces bright
colors.
2 Thread them onto colored string.

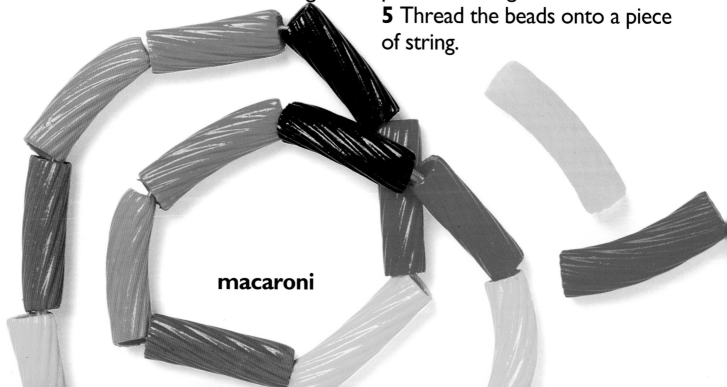

macaroni

Get set, go!
Salt Dough Beads

1 Put 2 cups of flour, 1 cup of salt, and 1 cup of water into a large mixing bowl. Mix the dough together until it forms a ball.

2 Put the ball on a floured surface and knead it with your hands until it is smooth. Break off small pieces of dough and roll them between your palms to make beads.

3 Use a toothpick or knitting needle to make holes through them.

salt dough

4 Ask a grown-up to put the beads on a baking tray and bake them in the oven for about half an hour at a low temperature. When they are cold you can paint them and thread them onto a piece of string.

Cover Up

Sometimes we need special clothes to protect us. For example, if someone is doing a dangerous job, such as welding, she will wear a mask to protect her eyes from the bright light and heat.

Astronauts wear spacesuits that cover their heads and bodies completely. When they are on the moon's surface the suits allow them to breathe and move around easily. Their boots are weighted to keep the astronauts from floating away.

Some sports can be dangerous. The ice hockey player in the photograph is wearing a mask and helmet to protect his face and head, and pads on his arms and legs. Bicyclists wear special helmets in case they fall. This skateboarder is wearing a helmet, gloves, and pads over long sleeves and pants.

Quiz

1 What kind of clothes are these?

3 What kind of fabric are the clothes in this picture made of?

2 What are these beads made of?

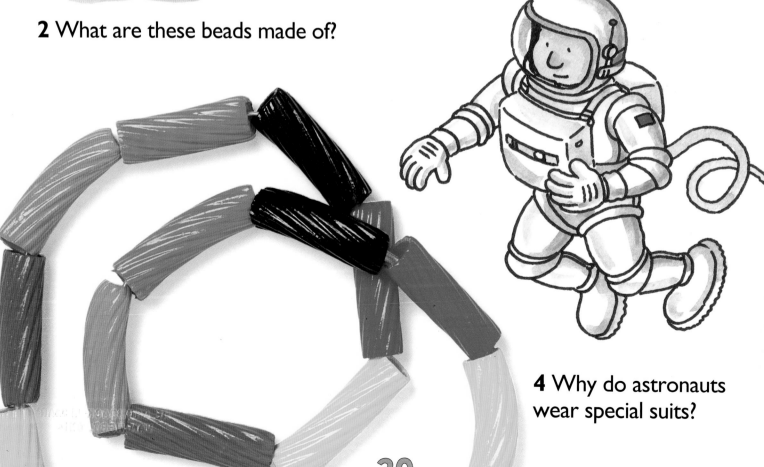

4 Why do astronauts wear special suits?

5 What is this man doing?

7 What is this fluffy stuff?

6 What is this white juice made into?

Answers on page 32.

Index

astronaut 28

balloons 19

beads 26, 27

cardboard 6, 7, 10, 11, 14

cocoon 12

cotton 8, 14

fabric 2, 4, 5, 8, 12, 14, 15

fabric paint 10, 11

festivals 20

headdress 21, 25

ice hockey 28

jewelry 24, 25

knitting 15

latex 18

mask 22

national costume 20

necklace 25

pads 28

paper 16, 17, 22

pom-poms 6, 7

rubber 18, 19

shearer 4

sheep 4, 5

silk 12, 13, 14

silkworm 12

sponge 10, 11

T-shirt 10, 11

waterproof 18

weaving 4, 14, 15, 16, 17

wool 4, 5, 6, 7, 14

yarn 14, 15, 25

Photo credits: cover, p. 12, p. 24-25 Spectrum Colour Library; p. 2-3 Pictures Colour Library; p. 5, p. 9, p. 19 Tony Stone Worldwide; p. 4, p. 6-7, p. 8, p. 10-11, p. 12-13, p. 14-15, p. 16-17, p. 18, p. 22-23, p. 24-25 (background), p. 26-27 Steve Shott; p. 13, p. 21 Britstock–IFA; p. 28 Image Bank

First published in the United States in 1994 by
Thomson Learning, 115 Fifth Avenue, New York, NY 10003

First published in 1994 by Two-Can Publishing Ltd.
Copyright © 1994 Two-Can Publishing Ltd.

Printed and bound in Hong Kong

Library of Congress Cataloging-in-Publication Data

James, Diane.
    What we wear/Diane James & Sara Lynn; illustrated by Joe Wright.
        p. cm. – (Play and discover)
    Includes index.
    ISBN 1-56847-143-2
    1. Clothing and dress – Juvenile literature. 2. Handicraft – Juvenile literature.
    3. Textile fabrics – Juvenile literature. [1. Clothing and dress. 2. Handicraft. 3. Textiles.]
    I. Lynn, Sara. II. Wright, Joe, ill. III. Title. IV. Series: Play and discover series.
    TT507.J36   1994
    646'.3 – dc20   94-5756

Answers to Quiz
p. 30-31

1 Dutch.

2 Dry macaroni.

3 Cotton.

4 So that they can breathe and walk on the surface of the moon.

5 Shearing sheep.

6 Rubber.

7 Wool.

PLAY & DISCOVER books
What We Eat ◆ Rain & Shine
◆ What We Wear ◆ Growing Up